A Note to Parents

You can help your Level 3 reader.

★ Keep up the habit of reading aloud with your older child. For many years, your child's listening comprehension will be greater than his or her ability to read alone.

★ Make reading with your child interactive. Try taking turns—you read one page, your child reads the next. Sit side by side.

★ Let your child read aloud the main character's part, while you read the other parts. This technique will help improve your child's comprehension, expression, and fluency.

Extend and enhance the reading experience.

★ Build background knowledge by relating this book to other books your child has read.

★ Find new books on topics your child likes, such as space travel or wild animals. Choose different kinds of books, including poetry, biography, and fiction.

★ Visit a museum, zoo, or theater to enrich current interests and discover new ones.

★ Be a role model. Let your child see you reading. Share your enjoyment by reading aloud fantastic phrases or humorous tidbits.

★ As your child becomes a fluent reader and prefers to read alone, provide a quiet, comfortable reading corner.

Most of all, enjoy your reading time together!

—Bernice Cullinan, Ph.D.,
Professor of Reading, New York University

To Tom and Elizabeth, with thanks
for our many great adventures
—RLH

To the constant joys of my life,
Ann, Erik, and Elizabeth
—GSG

Many thanks to Dr. Valerie Neal of the National Air and Space
Museum for reviewing the text and artwork for this book.

Reader's Digest Children's Books
Reader's Digest Road, Pleasantville, NY 10570-7000
Copyright © 2000 Reader's Digest Children's Publishing, Inc.
All rights reserved. Reader's Digest Children's Books and All-Star Readers are
trademarks and Reader's Digest is a registered trademark
of The Reader's Digest Association, Inc.
Printed in Hong Kong
10 9 8 7 6 5 4 3 2 1

Library of Congress Cataloging-in-Publication Data is available.

LIFTOFF!
A Space Adventure

by Rosanna Hansen
illustrated by George Gaadt

3

All-Star Readers™

Reader's Digest Children's Books™
Pleasantville, New York • Montréal, Québec

How would it feel to fly into space?

What do astronauts do on a shuttle trip?

Come aboard and let's find out!

It's early morning at the Kennedy Space Center. You are strapped in your seat on the space shuttle. Six other astronauts sit near you. Five minutes until liftoff!

While you wait for liftoff, you think about the way the shuttle is made. The orbiter is the main part of the shuttle. The other parts are the solid rocket boosters and the outer, or external, fuel tank.

The shuttle can fly into space over 100 times. It goes up like a rocket and lands like a glider plane.

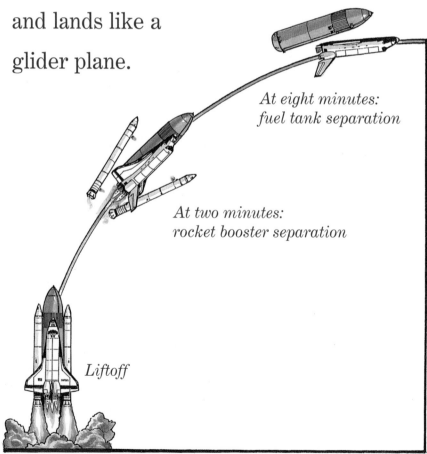

At eight minutes: fuel tank separation

At two minutes: rocket booster separation

Liftoff

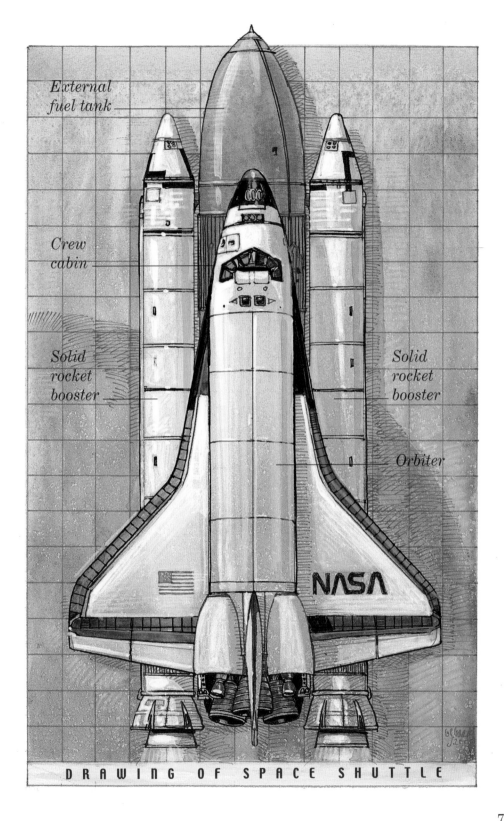

External
fuel tank

Crew
cabin

Solid
rocket
booster

Solid
rocket
booster

Orbiter

NASA

DRAWING OF SPACE SHUTTLE

At last the final countdown begins.
"Ten seconds…nine...eight…seven…"
With a roar, the three main engines fire.
"Four…three…two…ONE!" With a
louder roar, the two rocket boosters fire.
Clouds of exhaust rise through the air.
The shuttle blasts up from the
launch platform.

"Liftoff! We have liftoff!" cheers
Mission Control.

As the shuttle rises, you begin to shake up and down. Your heart pounds loudly. You feel a little scared.

As the shuttle goes faster, you are pushed down hard in your seat. This heaviness, or pressure, is called a G-force. You feel like you have a rock on your chest. Your whole body feels heavier and heavier.

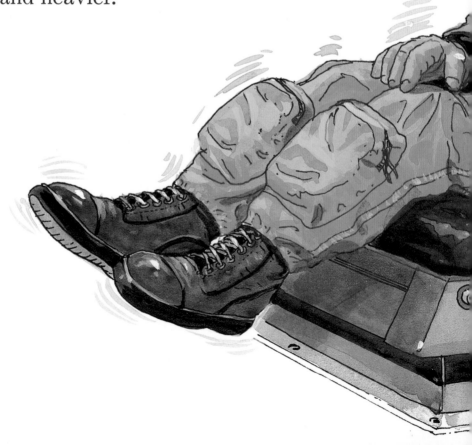

BOOM! The rocket boosters fall away.
Suddenly, the rock on your chest is gone.
You feel as light as a feather. You have
entered space!

THUMP! The fuel tank falls away. You
are almost 200 miles above Earth. Soon
the shuttle will begin to orbit, or circle,
Earth. Moving through space so fast
overcomes the pull of gravity. Without the
normal pull of gravity, you feel very light.
We call this lightness micro-gravity, ·
or weightlessness.

Oops! There goes your pen, floating by your head. Better grab it before it gets away. Everything floats in micro-gravity. Food, tools, books, even you—everything not tied down will start to float.

Your hair floats out from your head and is hard to brush. You can't take a shower—the water would float away. Instead, you wash with a wet cloth. Going to the bathroom is different, too. You use a special toilet that sucks the waste down. And you have to wear a seat belt to stay in place on the toilet.

In micro-gravity, your body changes. The blood and other fluids move from your legs to your upper body. This makes your face puffy. Your nose feels stuffed up. Your spine stretches, and you actually grow an inch taller!

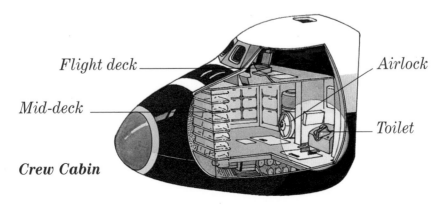

Flight deck

Airlock

Mid-deck

Toilet

Crew Cabin

During this space trip, your team has an important job. You will help build a section of the International Space Station, or ISS. First, your team flies the shuttle alongside the ISS. Then you and your teammate get ready to work outside the shuttle.

Before you can go outside, you must put on your space suit. It has pants, a top, gloves, boots, and a helmet. The space suit keeps you safe. It protects you from the extreme heat and cold of space. And it has air for you to breathe.

On Earth, the suit is heavy and bulky.

In space, it is light and easier to put on.

Ready? Let's go!

As you leave the shuttle, you step out
into…NOTHING! There is nothing but
empty space below your feet. Luckily, you
both have your jetpacks. You steer with
the help of joysticks.

You jet over to the ISS work site.

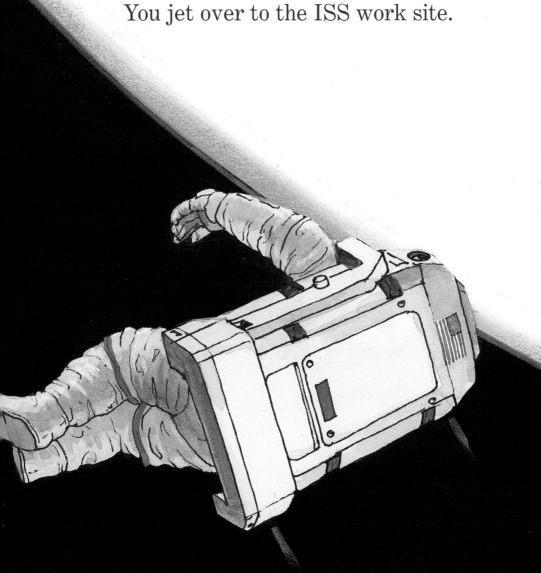

Today you are going to install a new
solar panel on the ISS. Solar panels soak
up light from the sun and turn it into
electricity. You reach for your space
tools and get to work.

Good job! It took awhile, but the new
solar panel is in place at last. You hook
your tools to your waist and head
back to the shuttle.

After you take your space suit off, it's time to fix dinner. What's on the menu? How about turkey, pasta, fruit salad, and pudding? Some of the food is dried. You just add water and heat it up. Then you fasten the food packs onto your tray.

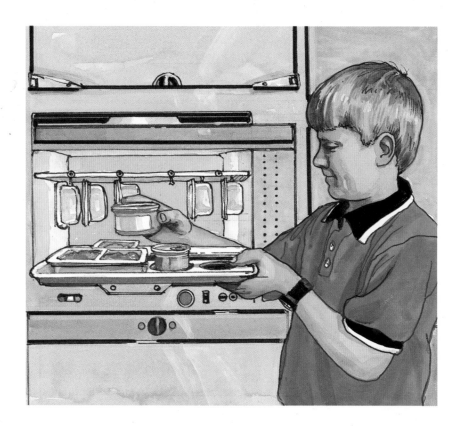

Oops! Someone left the fruit bin open. Catch the fruit before it floats off and makes a mess!

Dinnertime on the shuttle can be exciting—especially when the food won't stay put. Once the apples and oranges are stored away, you can finally settle down to eat.

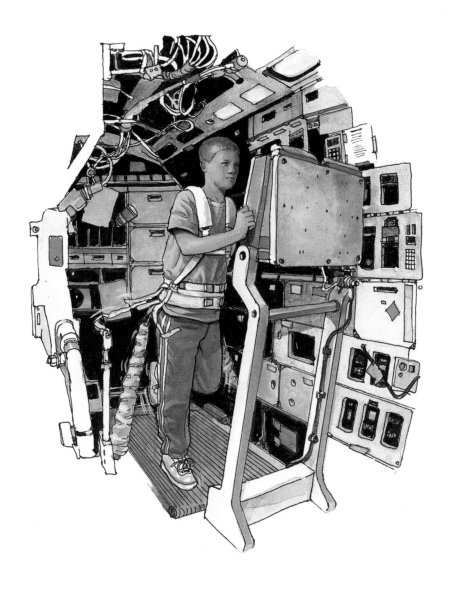

An hour after dinner, it is time to exercise. You need to exercise every day in space. Without exercise, your body would get weak. You might start to feel tired or sick.

Finally, it's time to relax. Would you like to read or play games? No! You want to look out the window, like everybody else. You take turns looking at faraway Earth. It looks beautiful against the inky black of space.

As the shuttle speeds along, you can see Earth's oceans and land zip by. The dark blue parts are ocean. The brown parts are land, and the swirling white is cloud cover.

Every 90 minutes, the shuttle makes a full orbit around Earth. That means you have 45 minutes of daylight and then 45 minutes of night! During night, you can sometimes see lightning storms and the lights of large cities below.

Soon it is time for bed. You brush your teeth with special toothpaste that you can swallow. Then you get into your sleeping bag, which is strapped to the wall. The straps keep you from floating around and bumping into things.

You can sleep upside down or sideways if you wish. In space, it's comfortable whichever way you like.

After five days in space, your team has completed its work on the ISS. The new section of the station is finished.

It's time to return to Earth. Everyone packs up the tools and gear. One more look out the window—then you strap yourself into your seat.

Small engines called thrusters turn the shuttle around. Here goes!

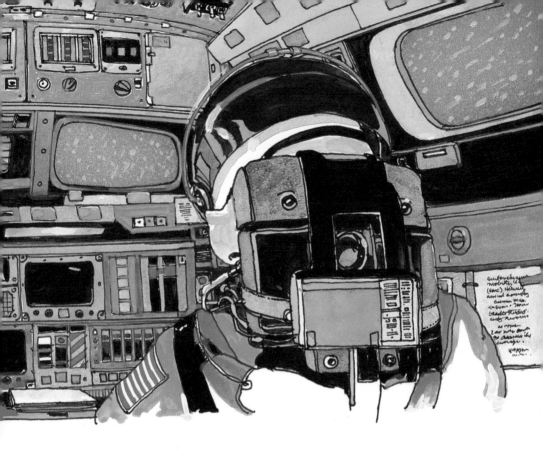

You slow down to begin the plunge toward Earth. Everything on the shuttle starts to shake.

You re-enter the blanket of air around Earth. The air rubs against the shuttle, making the outside fiery hot. All you see out the front window is a bright orange glow.

With its engines turned off, the shuttle zooms down. Here comes the runway! The drag parachute opens to slow down the spacecraft. THUMP! The main wheels touch down first, then the nose wheels. The shuttle brakes hard and rolls to a stop.

Hooray—you're home!

After landing, your body feels heavy and strange. You need to stay in the cabin for a while. You have to get used to the

pull of Earth's gravity again. Also, dangerous fuel needs to be drained from the shuttle.

At last, you are ready to leave the shuttle and step down on Earth once more. First you will see your family and have a medical checkup. Then it's time for a shower—the first one in a week. You can hardly wait to fly into space again!

This shuttle mission was important. Your team helped build one section of the International Space Station. People from many lands are working together on the ISS. It will take many years and many shuttle missions to finish this huge job.

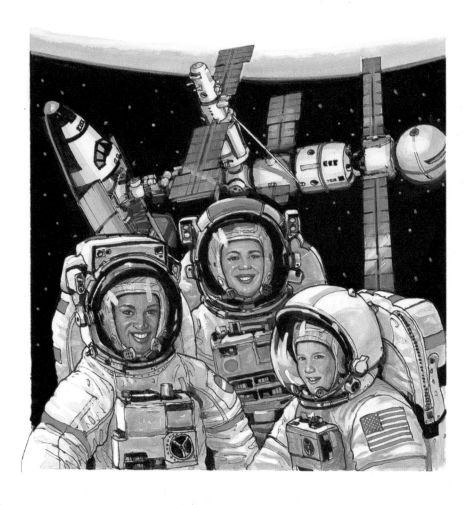

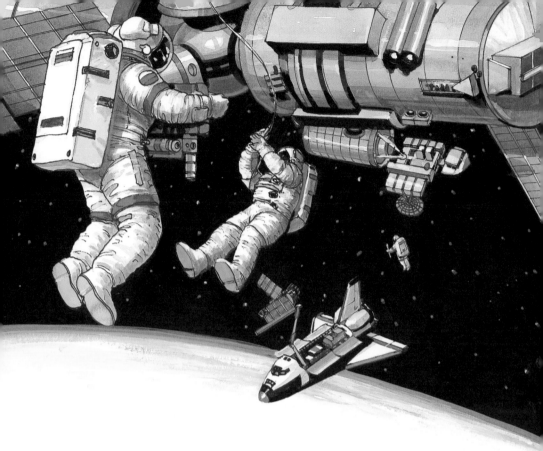

Why will it take so long to build the ISS? Imagine that you would like to build a big house a long way from home. You would have to carry all the materials for the house on your bicycle. That would take many long trips. Then, you would build one tiny room. You would live in that room for years while you worked on the rest of the house.

Building the International Space Station is something like that. The shuttle has to carry all the materials into space. This will take more than 40 shuttle trips in all.

Astronauts are now hard at work building the first part of the station. Soon, some astronauts will live in the part that is finished. From there, they will help build the rest of the station. They hope to finish the work by 2004.

When the station is done, it will be used for many things. It will hold special labs for scientists. And it may become a base for long space trips.

From the station, you might someday fly to the moon for a holiday. Or, perhaps you might fly off to Mars. Many years from now, your grandchildren might even leave the station to visit a planet in another galaxy, millions and millions of miles away.

Author's Note...

Everything you read in this book about going up in the space shuttle is true—except for one part. The part I imagined is that children your age are traveling into space. So far, no one your age has ridden in the shuttle. The youngest person to fly in the shuttle was Sally Ride. She was 32 years and 23 days old. In the future, though, children may very well fly into space. And some day, space travel may be as ordinary as going on a car trip with your parents.

Check Your Knowledge of Space Travel!

Place an All-Star sticker on the line under **T** *if the answer is true and under* **F** *if the answer is false.*

	T	F
1. The space shuttle circles Earth every 60 minutes.	_____	_____
2. The shuttle has two booster rockets.	_____	_____
3. In micro-gravity, everything that is not tied down will float.	_____	_____
4. In space you grow an inch taller.	_____	_____
5. People from many lands are working on the International Space Station.	_____	_____
6. The shuttle has two external fuel tanks.	_____	_____
7. The shuttle can land and be flown again, like an airplane.	_____	_____
8. The shuttle can fly into space over 500 times.	_____	_____
9. It's not necessary to exercise when you're in space.	_____	_____

Answers: 1-F; 2-T; 3-T; 4-T; 5-T; 6-F; 7-T; 8-F; 9-F